SADIQ
and the
Perfect Play

BY SIMAN NUURALI

ART BY ANJAN SARKAR

PICTURE WINDOW BOOKS
a capstone imprint

Sadiq is published by Picture Window Books,
an imprint of Capstone.
1710 Roe Crest Drive
North Mankato, Minnesota 56003
www.capstonepub.com

Library of Congress Cataloging-in-Publication Data is available on the
Library of Congress website.

ISBN: 978-1-5158-7101-9 (hardcover)
ISBN: 978-1-5158-7287-0 (paperback)
ISBN: 978-1-5158-7133-0 (eBook pdf)

Summary: Sadiq's big sister, Aliya, was recently cast in a community
theater musical. When Sadiq and his friends hear her practicing, they
decide to put on their own play for their friends and family. Sadiq
volunteers to be the director, but when he makes decisions without
his friends' input, everyone starts to get annoyed. Can they resolve
their issues before the big performance?

Design Element: Shutterstock/Irtsya

Designer: Brann Garvey

TABLE OF CONTENTS

HI, I'M SADIQ! MY FAMILY AND I LIVE IN MINNESOTA, BUT MY PARENTS ARE FROM SOMALIA. SOMETIMES WE SPEAK SOMALI AT HOME.

I'D LIKE YOU TO MEET MY FAMILY AND LEARN SOME INTERESTING FACTS AND TERMS FROM OUR CULTURE.

FACTS ABOUT SOMALIA

- Somalia is a coastal country in the Horn of Africa. It is about as big as Texas.

- Many Somalis are nomadic. That means they travel from place to place. They search for water, food, and land for their animals.

- Somalia is mostly desert. It doesn't rain often there.

- The camel is an important animal to Somali people. Camels can survive a long time without food or water.

- Around ninety-nine percent of all Somalis are Muslim.

SOMALI TERMS

baba (BAH-baah)—a common word for father

hooyo (HOY-yoh)—mother

qalbi (KUHL-bee)—my heart

salaam (sa-LAHM)—a short form of Arabic greeting, used by many Muslims. It also means "peace."

wiilkeyga (wil-KAY-gaah)—my son

CHAPTER 1

SINGING SURPRISE

It was a Saturday afternoon during spring break. Sadiq, Zaza, and Manny were bored. They had played video games all morning in the basement.

Upstairs, Sadiq's big sister, Aliya, was singing. She had been singing for at least twenty minutes. It was getting annoying.

"Ugh! She's been singing forever!" groaned Zaza.

"Why is she singing?" asked Manny.

Sadiq sighed. "She's in a musical next week. She's been practicing."

The boys were tired of playing video games. They decided to go upstairs.

"*Salaam*, everyone!" Sadiq called as he entered the living room.

"Salaam, boys," said Baba. "Why don't you sit with us? We can watch Aliya practice for her part in *Annie*."

Sadiq, Manny, and Zaza glanced at one another. They didn't really want to watch Aliya, but they knew they didn't have a choice. They sat on the couch.

Sadiq was sure he would find his sister's singing annoying. But as she started her next song, she sounded great!

"The sun will come out tomorrow!" Aliya sang. When she finished the song, she took a bow.

"You're really good," Hooyo said to her.

"That was a great performance, Aliya," said Baba.

"Thank you, Baba!" replied Aliya. "I've been working really hard to hit all the right notes."

"So good!" shouted Rania, clapping.

"Singing!" shouted Amina while turning in a circle.

"Your mom is right," Zaza whispered to Sadiq. "I couldn't tell earlier because we were so far away, but Aliya sounds really good."

"I wish I was in a play too," said Manny. "It looks like a lot of fun."

"Me too," replied Sadiq.

"We've never had a play at school," said Zaza sadly.

"What if we started our own theater club?" asked Sadiq.

"That's a great idea, Sadiq!" said Zaza.

"You will need a director," Aliya chimed in. She was listening to them talk. "I would volunteer, but I'm too busy with my role in *Annie.*"

"What does the director do?" Sadiq asked.

"The director makes the decisions!" Aliya said. "He or she is in charge of telling people where to go on stage. Sometimes they assign roles and find costumes."

"That sounds fun!" said Sadiq. "I will volunteer to be the director of our play."

"Cool," said Zaza. "What should we call our club?"

"How about the Friends Theater Club?" asked Manny.

"Awesome!" said Sadiq. He couldn't wait to get started as the director of the perfect play.

* * *

The next morning, Zaza and Manny met Sadiq at his house. They went outside and walked toward the park. As they got close to the swings, they saw three of their friends.

"Hi!" Sadiq called.

"Hi, guys!" replied Grayson, Zahra, and Dani.

"We're starting a theater club. Do you want to join?" asked Zaza.

"What will you do?" Dani asked.

"We're putting on a play. I just thought of it yesterday!" said Sadiq.

"We *all* thought of it," said Manny. He scrunched up his nose.

"What play should we do?" asked Zaza.

"How about *The Three Little Pigs*?" asked Manny.

"Ew!" Sadiq laughed. "Who wants to wear a pig costume?"

"What about *The Princess and the Pea*?" asked Dani. "It's the story of a lost girl who goes to a castle. A prince lives at the castle. He has been looking for a princess to marry, but he has not found anyone. The girl says she is a princess, but no one believes her."

"How does she convince them?" Zahra asked.

"The prince's mother, the queen, puts a pea under twenty mattresses to test her," Dani said. "If the girl feels the pea while she sleeps, she must be a princess."

"That sounds like a great story for a play," said Zaza. "What other characters are there?"

"There's a king, an announcer, and a court jester too," said Dani. "It has the perfect number of parts for our club!"

"Let's vote," said Zaza. "We can choose between *The Three Little Pigs* and *The Princess and the Pea*."

"I've decided we should do *The Princess and the Pea*. We will perform it here in the park," said Sadiq.

"But we didn't vote—" started Manny.

"I'll say who will play each part. Aliya said that's the director's job," said Sadiq.

"But Sadiq, we should *all* choose which part we like," said Zaza, frowning.

"The director of the play gets to decide," Sadiq said.

Manny looked at Zaza and shook his head sadly.

"I would really like to be the princess," said Dani.

"That's fine. But I will choose who plays the other parts," said Sadiq.

"I would like to be the queen," said Zahra.

"Can I be the court jester?" asked Manny.

"No. Zaza will be the jester because he's silly," said Sadiq. "Zahra will be the queen. Grayson will be the king. Manny, you can be the announcer. You'll tell the king and queen who is coming to visit them. That leaves me to be the prince."

"But I want to be the jester," said Manny.

"Zaza is the jester," said Sadiq. He put his hands on his hips.

Dani stared at Sadiq. "Why do you get to be the director *and* the prince?" she asked. "That doesn't seem fair."

"We have six characters in the play. There are six of us. We each play a part," Sadiq said simply. "Anyway, let's meet at my house tomorrow and plan."

Manny looked upset. The rest of the kids didn't know what to say. They nodded and started walking back to their homes.

CHAPTER 2

BUILDING THE SET

The Friends Theater Club gathered at Sadiq's house on Monday for their next meeting.

Sadiq held a notebook and pencil in his lap. "Okay, what will we need for the play?" he asked.

"We have to build a set and find props to use," said Zaza.

"We need a script," Dani said.

"We also need costumes," said Manny.

"I have some princess gowns. My sister and I used them last Halloween," said Zahra.

Sadiq scribbled in his notebook. "Can you guys slow down?" he asked, frowning. "I can't answer and write at the same time!"

"My dad is a carpenter," said Grayson. "I can ask if he'll help us build the set."

"That would be great, Grayson!" Zahra said.

The kids continued to plan their perfect play. They went on Nuurali's computer and found a script. Then they printed out copies on Baba's printer. They ran through their lines.

After a while, Hooyo called Sadiq. It was time for dinner and for the rest of the club to go home.

Later that night, Grayson called Sadiq. "My dad said you guys can come over tomorrow," Grayson said. "We can start building the set! He said he has enough supplies for it."

"Awesome!" Sadiq said. "See you tomorrow!"

* * *

"Hi, kids!" said Mr. Sederstrom when the club arrived at Grayson's the next day. "How can I help you today?"

Everyone looked at Sadiq as they walked into the garage.

"I . . . I'm not sure," said Sadiq. "I made a list of what we need for our set."

"Let's take a look at it," Mr. Sederstrom said. Sadiq handed him the list.

"Castle walls, thrones, a door, tables, decorations . . ." Mr. Sederstrom read. "This all seems simple enough!"

Sadiq smiled. He was glad to have some help. "Should we start on the castle wa—" he started.

"Sadiq, how many people will come see the play?" interrupted Manny.

Sadiq didn't reply. He wanted to finish what he was saying. He took a breath and asked Mr. Sederstrom, "Should we start on the castle walls and then make the door?"

"That sounds like a good plan," Mr. Sederstrom said. He gathered wood from behind his workbench. "Zaza and Manny, could you please help me with this?"

Zaza and Manny agreed.

Then Mr. Sederstrom showed Grayson an old door he had at the back of his workshop. "Maybe you can use this on your set," he said.

"Can I paint it blue?" Grayson asked the group. He held up a can of paint he'd found.

"No, the door has to be red," said Sadiq.

"Okay. . . ." said Grayson. He searched the workshop for red paint. "Zahra and Dani, can you help me paint?"

The girls agreed.

Mr. Sederstrom went back to the workbench. He asked Zaza and Manny for help measuring the wood pieces.

Sadiq put down his notebook and went to help too. They helped Mr. Sederstrom measure and sand the wood. Then they helped him glue the walls together.

Grayson, Zahra, and Dani painted the door. When they were done, there was still plenty to do. Sadiq and Manny made posters. They would hang them around the neighborhood to get people to come to the play.

Zahra and Dani made crowns for the queen, king, and prince out of cardboard. Zaza and Grayson collected old furniture from around the workshop. They found chairs, tables, and decorations to use on set.

When it was time to go home, Sadiq reminded everyone to practice their lines. "We will go over them tomorrow at our first rehearsal!" he said.

CHAPTER 3

REHEARSALS

The next day, the group met in Sadiq's basement to practice.

"Does everyone have their costume?" asked Sadiq.

At first, nobody answered.

"We thought you were in charge of that," said Manny.

"Why?" asked Sadiq, looking confused.

"Because you've been in charge of everything else," said Zaza.

"You haven't listened to any of our ideas," added Manny.

"Fine," mumbled Sadiq. "I will figure out the costumes. But right now, let's practice. Does everyone have a script?"

The club members nodded.

"Great. We can go through our lines. Grayson, you and I will sit here," said Sadiq. He pointed to two chairs in the middle of the room. "Zaza, as the jester, you'll be silly and make us laugh."

Zaza nodded and got into position.

"Manny, you will stand by the door," said Sadiq. "You'll blow a trumpet to get everyone's attention."

"Is there a trumpet I can use?" asked Manny.

Sadiq shook his head. "Not yet. You will have to pretend for now."

"Do I get a jester's hat?" asked Zaza.

"Not right now. We have to find our spots first," said Sadiq.

"Sadiq, should I sit next to Grayson?" asked Zahra.

"Just a second, Zahra," said Sadiq. He turned to Dani and pointed to the corner. "You can stand here until Manny announces you."

"What lines should I practice?" asked Manny.

Sadiq walked back to Manny. "Your lines start here," he said. He pointed to the script.

"Zahra, you sit next to Grayson," said Sadiq.

"But where?" asked Zahra.

"Your chairs will be next to each other," said Sadiq. He moved another chair to the center of the room.

"Sadiq—" Zahra started.

"WHAT?!" shouted Sadiq. He stomped his foot. "Do I have to do everything?"

Everyone went quiet. Then Zahra spoke up. "I want to go home," she said.

"That was really mean, Sadiq," said Zaza quietly.

"You were all talking to me. You were all asking for help at the same time!" said Sadiq, pouting.

"I'm going home," said Manny.

"Me too," said Dani. She was holding Zahra's hand.

Without another word, Sadiq's friends all left. Sadiq was alone. He slumped onto a chair. "Why do I have to do everything?" he huffed.

After a few minutes, Baba came downstairs. "What happened to our famous actors?" he asked.

Sadiq didn't answer.

Baba put a hand on Sadiq's shoulder. "Is everything okay, Sadiq?"

"I have to think about the set. I have to figure out costumes," Sadiq said, his voice rising. "And now everyone's mad at me."

"Did you ask for help?" asked Baba.

"No," replied Sadiq. "Aliya said the director makes all the decisions."

"It sounds like you could use some help," said Baba. "Why don't you talk to your friends?"

"Maybe," Sadiq said.

"Things will seem better tomorrow after you get rest, *wiilkeyga*," said Baba. "Let's go eat dinner."

"Yes, Baba," said Sadiq, but he didn't believe it.

How will I direct the perfect play? thought Sadiq. He dragged his feet as he followed his father upstairs.

CHAPTER 4

ALIYA'S MUSICAL

The next day, Sadiq was in his room when a thought came to him. *I need to ask Hooyo for help with the costumes.*

Sadiq walked to his parents' bedroom. "I need help, Hooyo," he said.

"What can I help you with, *qalbi*?" Hooyo asked.

"I don't have costumes for our play," Sadiq explained. "Or anything else. We still need a trumpet and a bed for the set. I don't know how I'll get it all done."

"Well, right now we have to go see your sister perform in her musical," said Hooyo.

"But Hooyo, I have a lot to do," said Sadiq.

"Qalbi, you've known about your sister's musical. She'll be very sad if you don't come," said Hooyo.

"But if I don't get all these things done, the play will be ruined," said Sadiq. "I don't want to let my friends down."

"Sadiq, it's important to keep our promises," replied Hooyo. "We can talk when we get back, okay?"

"Okay, Hooyo," said Sadiq, looking down.

* * *

Sadiq and his family arrived at the theater. People were already in their seats. The curtains were drawn across the stage. Soon the lights were turned down.

"This is a great turnout!" whispered Baba.

"Yes," said Hooyo. "How exciting!"

A man came onstage. "Welcome!" he said into the microphone. "My name is John Anderson. I am the director of Valley Street Community Theater. Thank you for coming. We hope you enjoy our production of *Annie*!"

The curtains went up. The stage came into view. In the front there were four untidy beds. Several girls gathered around them. Sadiq could see Aliya standing beside one of the beds.

The musical began. Sadiq was excited. The other kids were good singers, but he thought Aliya was the best!

I wonder where they got the beds, thought Sadiq. He nodded along to the music. *We need a bed for the princess in our play!*

Before Sadiq knew it, the play had ended. Everyone stood up to cheer!

Sadiq's family went to find Aliya. The twins jumped up and down and called for Aliya. Finally they spotted her in the crowd and ran to her.

"Wonderful job, Aliya!" Hooyo said.

"You did great!" Sadiq said. He hugged his sister.

The director came over to introduce himself. "You must be Aliya's family," he said. "It's nice to meet you all. I just wanted to say that Aliya is very talented. She has been a joy to direct."

"Oh, thank you!" said Baba and Hooyo together.

"This is Nuurali, Sadiq, Rania, and Amina," said Baba. "Sadiq recently formed a theater club with his friends. They'll be putting on *The Princess and the Pea* soon."

"Fantastic! How is that going?" asked Mr. Anderson.

"Not very well," replied Sadiq. "Nobody knows their lines. I still have to figure out our costumes and props. I'm the director. I have to do it all myself."

"Theater directors aren't in charge of *everything*. You can't do it all by yourself," said Mr. Anderson. "Part of being a director is learning how to delegate."

"What does *delegate* mean?" asked Sadiq.

"It means you ask for help. You can ask your friends to do certain tasks," said Mr. Anderson.

"Do *you* do that?" asked Sadiq, his eyes going wide.

Mr. Anderson smiled. "Of course! I wouldn't be able to do it all on my own. A set designer is in charge of the set. There is a costume designer who puts together all the costumes."

"Thank you, Mr. Anderson!" said Sadiq. "I can't wait to ask my friends for help."

CHAPTER 5

HELP ARRIVES

When Sadiq got home from Aliya's play, he called his friends. The club agreed to meet at the park the next day.

"I'm sorry for being mean," Sadiq said when his friends arrived. "I should have asked for help. Instead I was trying to do everything myself."

"We didn't think you wanted help," said Zaza.

Manny nodded. "You wanted to do everything."

"You got really bossy," said Zaza.

"I am sorry," said Sadiq sadly, looking down. "I wanted the play to be perfect. I thought directors needed to do it all. But I need help. Could someone take care of the costumes?"

"I'll see what my sister has in her dress-up bin," Dani said. "Zahra can help me."

"My dad said he can help with the rest of the set pieces," said Grayson.

"I can ask my brother for his trumpet," said Manny. "Zaza and I will try to find other props too."

"Thank you," said Sadiq. "I didn't know putting on a play would be so hard."

"We don't mind helping, Sadiq," said Manny.

Zahra nodded. "Next time, we can all agree on a plan from the start."

"Thank you!" said Sadiq. "You guys are awesome!" He gave them each a hug.

"Okay," he said after a moment. "Now let's start practicing. Zahra and Grayson, you're over here. Dani, don't come in until Manny announces you."

Now that he had some help, Sadiq enjoyed directing the play.

"Manny, you'll have to be really loud when you're announcing the princess," said Sadiq.

Manny held a stick up to his face. He pretended it was the trumpet. He pursed his lips to blow.

They practiced until everyone knew their lines.

"I think we should go home. We need to get started on the other tasks," said Dani.

"Yes, you are right," said Sadiq. "We have a lot of work to do before Sunday. Thank you all for helping me."

"That's what friends are for!" said Zaza. He crossed his eyes and made faces at Sadiq.

Sadiq laughed. "You really are the court jester, Zaza!"

CHAPTER 6

SHOWTIME!

The theater club was finally going to present their play to the neighborhood!

"Sadiq, are these the sleeping pads you wanted to use?" asked Baba.

"Yes, Baba," replied Sadiq.

"Do you have a pea?" asked Nuurali.

"I'm using one of my marbles," replied Sadiq.

"Where are the rest of your set pieces?" asked Baba.

"Mr. Sederstrom has most of them," Sadiq said. "He will bring them to the park. Thank you, Baba!"

When Sadiq got to the park with his family, everyone was there.

Mr. Sederstrom was putting up the set pieces. The kids went to help him. He had let them borrow camping chairs. Zahra and Dani had put gold wrapping paper around them. They wanted to make them look like thrones. The kids placed the thrones on the set.

Many neighbors had come to the park to watch the play. Sadiq could hear people talking and laughing. He started to feel nervous!

The kids took their positions. Sadiq went to the front to introduce their play. "Hello, everyone!" he said. "Welcome to our play, *The Princess and the Pea*!"

The audience clapped and cheered. But they quickly went quiet so the play could start.

King Grayson, Queen Zahra, and Prince Sadiq were on stage. They discussed Prince Sadiq's quest to marry a real princess.

"Father," said Prince Sadiq, "I have searched all over the kingdom. I have not found a real princess to marry. They are either too short or too tall. Too quiet or too loud. Some have no manners at all! What am I to do?"

Suddenly there was a knock on the door. Manny, the announcer, entered the scene.

He blew his trumpet. Then he announced loudly, "There is a young woman at the door. She says she's a real princess!"

"We will test if she's honest!" said Queen Zahra.

Sadiq peeked out of the corner of his eye. The audience was smiling and enjoying themselves!

Finally the play came to an end. The cast of friends moved to the front and bowed.

There was clapping and whistling. People shouted, "Bravo!"

Once the cheering died down, Sadiq spoke up. "We would like to thank you for coming to see our play. I also want to thank my friends onstage. They practiced a lot. They also helped with the set and costumes!"

Everyone clapped again for the theater club. Then the audience members got up from their seats.

"Here you go, Sadiq," said Aliya, walking up to him. She handed her brother a bunch of flowers. "These are from all of us. You and the club did a wonderful job!"

"That was great, qalbi," said Hooyo. Baba nodded. They each gave him a hug.

Sadiq beamed. "You really think so?" he asked.

"Yes! But not as great as my performance in *Annie.* My musical was the best ever!" Aliya said.

Sadiq playfully stuck his tongue out at his sister. He knew that the Friends Theater Club had put on the perfect play!

GLOSSARY

costume (KOSS-toom)—clothes worn by actors

delegate (DEL-i-geyt)—to give another person a job or task

director (duh-REK-tur)—the person who is in charge of a show

interrupt (in-tuh-RUHPT)—to start talking before someone else has finished talking

jester (JES-tur)—a person kept in royal courts to amuse and entertain people

musical (MYOO-zuh-kuhl)—a show with singing and dancing

perform (pur-FORM)—to entertain an audience

production (pruh-DUHK-shuhn)—a play, movie, television show, or other form of entertainment that is presented to others

quest (KWEST)—an adventure in which a hero tries to achieve a goal

rehearsal (ri-HUR-suhl)—a practice, especially for a performance

trumpet (TRUHM-pit)—a brass musical instrument that consists of a long tube with a wide funnel shape at one end and that has valves by which different tones are produced

turnout (TURN-out)—the number of people at an event

untidy (uhn-TYE-dee)—messy

workshop (WURK-shop)—a room or other building where things are made or fixed

TALK ABOUT IT

1. Manny feels upset while the Friends Theater Club works on the play. Why do you think he was mad?

2. Mr. Anderson, the director of Aliya's play, tells Sadiq a director must ask others for help. Think of a time you've had to ask others for help on completing a project. How did you delegate or ask others to do certain tasks?

3. Baba and Hooyo help Sadiq with his problems in the story. What are some of the lessons they teach him as he puts his play together?

WRITE IT DOWN

1. Sadiq has trouble juggling all the duties of director. What are some of the hints that show Sadiq has taken on more jobs than he can handle? Make a list of two or three.

2. The Friends Theater Club learns that a lot of work goes into making a play. Write about what part of making a play you think you'd be best at.

3. Write a list of the differences between Sadiq's play and Aliya's play and how they were performed.

WRITE YOUR OWN PLAY!

Sadiq and his friends put a play together and perform it for their neighborhood. With a little writing and a lot of imagination, you can write your own play!

WHAT YOU NEED:

- a computer or tablet
- a printer
- paper
- writing utensil

WHAT TO DO:

1. Choose how you want to write your play. Do you want to write on paper, or would you rather type on a computer or tablet?

2. Come up with the characters! Who do you want to appear in your play? They can be whoever or whatever you want!

3. What do you want to happen to the characters in your play? What should they say to each other?

4. Once you have a good idea of who your characters are and what you want to happen in your play, start writing!

Here is an example of what a play script looks like:

Zara: We're starting a theater club. Do you want to join?

Dani: What will you do?

Sadiq: We're putting on a play. I just thought of it yesterday!

Manny: We all thought of it. (*Manny scrunches up his nose.*)

Zaza: What play should we do?

Manny: How about *The Three Little Pigs?*

Sadiq: Ew! Who wants to wear a pig costume?

5. Once you have your story written, it's time to act it out. You can have friends or family play the characters, or you can perform them yourself!

CREATORS

Siman Nuurali grew up in Kenya. She now lives in Minnesota. Siman and her family are Somali—just like Sadiq and his family! She and her five children love to play badminton and board games together. Siman works at Children's Hospital, and in her free time, she also enjoys writing and reading.

Anjan Sarkar is a British illustrator based in Sheffield, England. Since he was little, Anjan has always loved drawing stuff. And now he gets to draw stuff all day for his job. Hooray! In addition to the Sadiq series, Anjan has been drawing mischievous kids, undercover aliens, and majestic tigers for other exciting children's book projects.